Too Much Water!

An Ivy and Mack story

Written by Juliet Clare Bell

Illustrated by Gustavo Mazali

with Camilla Galindo

Collins

What's in this story?

Listen and say

 Download the audio at www.collins.co.uk/839657

water
dry
wet

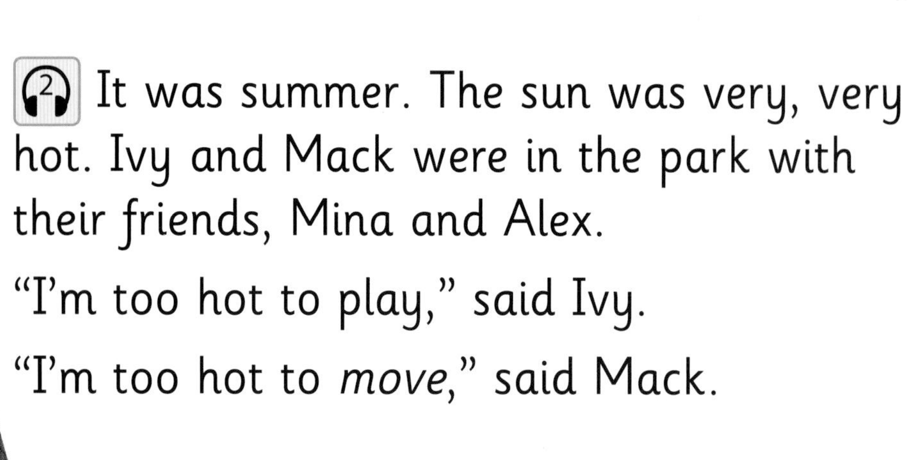

It was summer. The sun was very, very hot. Ivy and Mack were in the park with their friends, Mina and Alex.

"I'm too hot to play," said Ivy.

"I'm too hot to *move*," said Mack.

Mum looked at the children's hot faces.
"Are you OK?" she asked.

"We don't want to play in the park.
It's too hot!" said Ivy.

"Can we go home now?" asked Mack.

"Yes, let's all go home." said Mum.

"What are you doing?" said Mum. "Why don't you go and play in the garden?"

"I'm too hot!" said Ivy.

"So are we!" said Mack, Alex and Mina.

"I know," said Mack. "Let's put the tent up in the garden! We can play in it. It's too hot to play in the house."

"It's too hot to put the tent up," said Ivy.

Mack and Alex put the tent up.
"Can I help?" asked Mum.
"No, thank you," said Mack and Alex.

Ivy and Mina came to see the tent.

“It’s too hot in here!” said Ivy.

“Let’s get some ice cream,” said Mack.

Mack and Alex went to the kitchen.

“It’s too hot, Mum!” said Mack. “Have we got any ice cream?”

“I don’t know,” said Mum. “Go and look.”

Mack and Alex looked for ice cream.
"Oh no! There isn't any ice cream!"
said Mack.

But Alex saw some berries. "*These* are very cold," he said. "Why don't we eat some berries?"

"Mum, can we eat some berries?"
asked Mack.

"Where's the ice cream?" asked Ivy.

"There isn't any," said Mack.

"But there are berries," said Alex.

The berries were nice and cold.
"That's better!" said Ivy.

They ate all the berries. Mack went back to the kitchen.

Mack got cold water for everyone.
Then he saw a butterfly. It was beautiful.

He watched it fly … and then …

“MACK!” said Ivy.

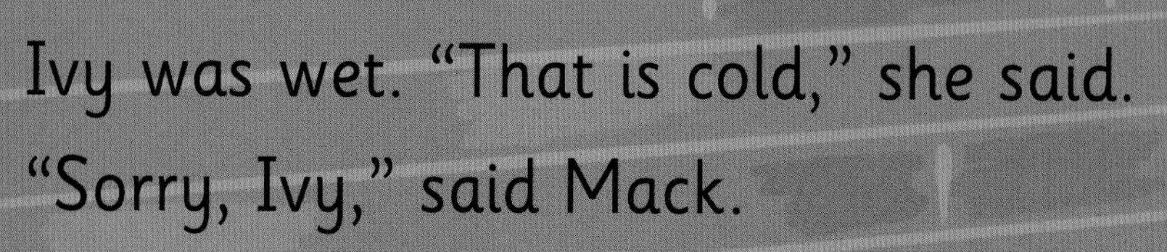

Ivy was wet. "That is cold," she said.

"Sorry, Ivy," said Mack.

Ivy laughed. "It's great. I'm not hot. And now I've got a good idea for a game!"

Mina and Ivy found some bottles and cups. Mum helped Mack and Alex. They got some buckets of water.

"OK, everyone!" said Ivy. "Now, one, two, three ... GO!"

Mack and Alex got wet. Ivy and Mina got wet. Everyone got *very* wet!

Ivy put more water in the buckets. “What do you think, Mack?”

“I think that’s *too* much water!”

"*Is* it too much?" asked Ivy.

Ivy and Mina picked up a bucket of water. *SPLASH!*

Mack and Alex picked up a bucket of water. *SPLASH!*

They laughed and laughed.

Then they stood in the sun and got dry.

Ivy, Mack, Mina and Alex got into the tent.

"This is fun," said Alex.

"What's that noise?" said Mack.

The noise got louder and louder ...

… and the tent got wetter and wetter.

"This *is* too much water!" said Ivy. "Quick! Run!"

Picture dictionary

Listen and repeat 

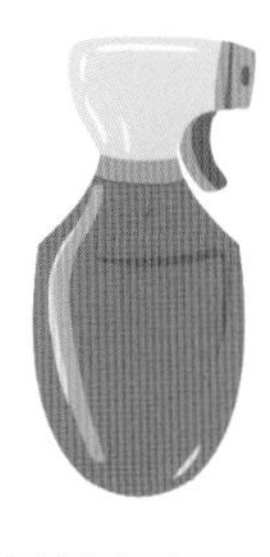

bottle

bucket

butterfly

summer

sun

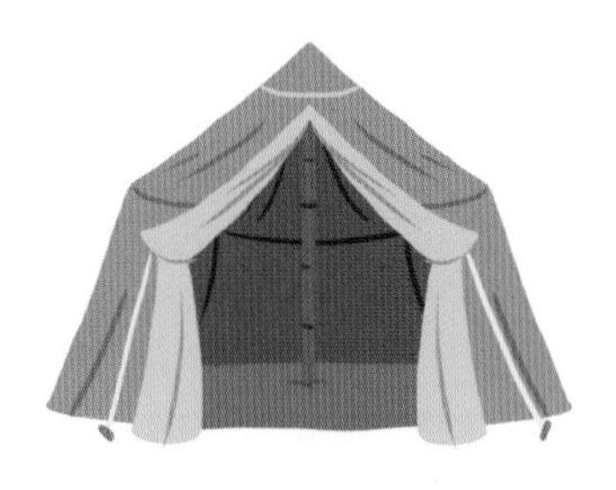

tent

1 Look and order the story

2 Listen and say  

Download a reading guide for parents and teachers at www.collins.co.uk/839657

Collins

Published by Collins
An imprint of HarperCollins*Publishers*
Westerhill Road
Bishopbriggs
Glasgow
G64 2QT

HarperCollins*Publishers*
1st Floor, Watermarque Building
Ringsend Road
Dublin 4
Ireland

William Collins' dream of knowledge for all began with the publication of his first book in 1819.

A self-educated mill worker, he not only enriched millions of lives, but also founded a flourishing publishing house. Today, staying true to this spirit, Collins books are packed with inspiration, innovation and practical expertise. They place you at the centre of a world of possibility and give you exactly what you need to explore it.

10 9 8 7 6 5 4 3 2

ISBN 978-0-00-839657-2

www.collins.co.uk/elt

British Library Cataloguing in Publication Data

A catalogue record for this publication is available from the British Library.

Author: Juliet Clare Bell
Lead illustrator: Gustavo Mazali (Beehive)
Copy illustrator: Camilla Galindo (Beehive)
Series editor: Rebecca Adlard
Commissioning editor: Zoë Clarke
Publishing manager: Lisa Todd
Product managers: Jennifer Hall and Caroline Green
In-house editor: Alma Puts Keren
Project manager: Emily Hooton
Editor: Deborah Friedland
Proofreaders: Natalie Murray and Michael Lamb
Cover designer: Kevin Robbins
Typesetter: 2Hoots Publishing Services Ltd
Audio produced by id audio, London
Reading guide author: Julie Penn
Production controller: Rachel Weaver
Printed and bound by: GPS Group, Slovenia

MIX
Paper from responsible sources
FSC™ C007454

This book is produced from independently certified FSC™ paper to ensure responsible forest management.

For more information visit: **www.harpercollins.co.uk/green**

Download the audio for this book and a reading guide for parents and teachers at www.collins.co.uk/839657